Master Hansel and Miss Gretel

OXFORD
UNIVERSITY PRESS

The children were putting on a play of Hansel and Gretel. Kipper was the narrator, but he kept missing out bits of the story.

'What about the bit with the stepmother?' asked Wilf.

'Yes, Hansel and Gretel hear her telling their father to lose them in the woods,' said Biff.

'… so they drop a trail of bread to help them find their way home,' continued Chip.

'I know, I know,' cried Kipper.

But Chip had had enough. 'I'll come back when you know the story,' he said.

'Yeah,' said Wilf, and he gave Kipper the piece of bread from the play. Chip, Wilf, Biff, and Wilma all went into the house.

'I DO know it!' Kipper shouted after them.

'Then why aren't you telling it in the right order?' asked Anneena.

I wish he'd tell it right, thought Floppy. I like breadcrumbs!

The key on Floppy's collar started to glow.

Suddenly, Kipper, Anneena, and Floppy were whisked into a vortex of sparkling colours and lights. They were flying round and round, faster and faster . . .

They found themselves in a huge forest, leaning against a tall tree. Anneena stood up. 'This way, come on,' she said.

But Kipper hadn't heard her and he and Floppy started following a different path.

'This is quite scary, isn't it, Anneena?' he said. But when he looked around Anneena was nowhere to be seen.

Kipper and Floppy continued walking through the thick bushes and leaves and eventually they saw a girl walking in the forest. 'Hey, there she is!' cried Kipper. 'Anneena!'

But when the girl turned round, it wasn't Anneena at all.
'Who's Anneena?' asked the girl.
'My friend,' replied Kipper. 'I've lost her.'
'We're lost too,' said the girl, as a boy approached them.

They introduced themselves. 'I'm Hansel,' said the boy.

'So you must be Gretel,' said Kipper. 'From the story.'

They needed Kipper's help to find their way home. Kipper was delighted. 'You have to drop breadcrumbs and get to the gingerbread house,' he said excitedly.

Hansel and Gretel looked at each other with puzzled expressions.

'Where's the bread your father gave you?' asked Kipper.

'We ate it, of course,' said Gretel.

Kipper remembered the bread Wilf had given him and pulled it out of his pocket. 'I've got some,' he said.

They made a trail of breadcrumbs through the forest, just like in the fairy tale. But after a while, Gretel stopped walking and pointed ahead. A look of dismay came over her. 'Oh, no! Look!' she cried. 'We've gone round in a circle.'

And sure enough, there was the start of the breadcrumb trail. 'Whoops,' said Kipper. 'I've just remembered! You should have dropped the breadcrumbs before you got lost.'

'Now he tells us,' Gretel muttered to Hansel.

Just then, Kipper heard a bird singing and glanced up. 'Look!' he said, as a beautiful white bird flew down and perched on a nearby branch. 'We have to follow it!' he cried, as the bird flew away.

So off they all ran, after the white bird, and before long they came to a clearing. And in the clearing was the gingerbread house. The children's eyes lit up as they looked at all the wonderful cakes and sweets the house was built from. It didn't take them long to start tucking into bits of the walls and window ledges!

An old lady looked out of the front door. 'Nibble, children, walls taste nice. Nibble, nibble, just like mice,' she said, and invited them into the house.

They followed her in, but as soon as she closed the front door behind them, she turned into an ugly old witch. 'I have you at my mercy!' she cackled loudly.

Then they heard another voice calling, 'Kipper! Help!' They looked around. It was Anneena! And she was locked in a big wooden cage!

The witch grabbed Hansel and Floppy and shoved them into the cage as well. 'That juicy girl looks good to munch. The smaller boy, I'll eat for lunch,' she said, laughing to herself.

The witch turned to look at Kipper and Gretel. 'You two,' she shouted. 'Get peeling!' So Kipper and Gretel set to work peeling a big pile of potatoes for the witch's stew. Gretel leaned towards Kipper. 'If you make the witch look the other way, I'll try and open the cage,' she whispered.

'That's not what happens,' replied Kipper.

Gretel was getting frustrated. 'Then what does happen?' she asked.

But before Kipper could answer, the witch had ordered Gretel to see whether the oven was hot enough.

'That's it!' Kipper said to himself. 'Gretel,' he whispered. 'Pretend you don't know how to open it!'

'But I do!' replied Gretel.

'Please!' begged Kipper. 'I was right about the gingerbread house, wasn't I?'

So Gretel agreed to go along with Kipper's plan.

'How do I open it?' Gretel asked the witch.

'Stupid child! Let the boy do it!' the witch scolded.

'Oh, er, I don't know how to open it either!' said Kipper.

The witch sighed and got up and went to open the oven herself.

Kipper gestured to Gretel – she knew what she had to do!

Just as the witch opened the oven door, Gretel gave her a big shove and pushed her into the hot oven. Kipper ran and quickly shut the door behind her.

'Aaaaaarrrrgh!' cried the witch.

As soon as the witch had gone, all the windows and doors swung open – including the cage door and the lid to a wooden chest.

'Well done, Kipper,' cried Anneena.

'We're free,' shouted Hansel.

'And rich,' said Gretel, as she looked into the chest. It was full of jewels and coins! 'All thanks to you, Kipper,' she told him gratefully.

Hansel reached into the chest and pulled out a gold chain. 'This is for you,' he said, handing the chain to Kipper.

'Wow, thanks!' said Kipper.

Anneena turned to look at Floppy. 'The key's glowing,' she said.

We're going, thought Floppy.

They were back in the Robinsons' garden. The others had come back from the house, and they were all rehearsing the play again.

'They gave the treasure to their father,' Kipper narrated. 'And they all lived happily ever after!'

All the children cheered.

'Well done, Kipper!' said Anneena.

'You got it all in the right order!' added Wilf.

Biff turned to Anneena. 'Can we do something else now?' she asked.
No way! thought Floppy, gobbling up the trail of breadcrumbs.
I want some more bread!

OXFORD
UNIVERSITY PRESS

Great Clarendon Street, Oxford OX2 6DP

Oxford University Press is a department of the University of Oxford.
It furthers the University's objective of excellence in research, scholarship,
and education by publishing worldwide in

Oxford New York

Athens Auckland Bangkok Bogotá Buenos Aires Calcutta
Cape Town Chennai Dar es Salaam Delhi Florence Hong Kong Istanbul
Karachi Kuala Lumpur Madrid Melbourne Mexico City Mumbai
Nairobi Paris São Paulo Shanghai Singapore Taipei Tokyo Toronto Warsaw

with associated companies in Berlin Ibadan

Oxford is a registered trade mark of Oxford University Press in the UK and in certain other countries

British Library Cataloguing in Publication Data available
ISBN 0-19-272476-2
1 3 5 7 9 10 8 6 4 2
Printed in Great Britain